W9-BQU-753

*1.00
9-18
CB

JUNE LAKE LIBRARY
Gift of CCAP

E   Chapouton, Anne-Marie
Cha   Billy Hte Brave
JLB   ISBN0-200-72885-7

DATE DUE			
~~JUN 8 '9~~			
~~AUG 27 '92~~			
FEB 1 5 2003			

First published in the United States, Great Britain, Canada,
Australia and New Zealand in 1986 by North-South Books, an
imprint of Rada Matija AG.

Distributed in the United States by
Holt, Rinehart and Winston, 383 Madison Avenue,
New York, New York, 10017.
Library of Congress Catalog Card Number 85-63307

ISBN 0-03-008019-3

Distributed in Great Britain by
Blackie and Son Ltd, Furnival House, 14—18 High Holborn,
London WC1V 6BX.
British Library Cataloguing in Publication Data

Chapouton, Anne-Marie
  Billy the brave.
  I. Title II. Claverie, Jean III. Jeremie
  Peur-de-rien. *English*
  843'.914[J] PZ7

ISBN 0-200-72885-7

Distributed in Canada by
Douglas & McIntyre Ltd., Toronto.
Canadian Cataloguing in Publication Data available in
Marc Record from National Library of Canada.
ISBN 0 88894 766 6

Distributed in Australia and New Zealand by
Buttercup Books Pty. Ltd., Melbourne.
ISBN 0 949447 23 4

Printed in Germany

Billy the Brave

ANNE-MARIE CHAPOUTON/PICTURES BY JEAN CLAVERIE
TRANSLATED BY ANTHEA BELL

NORTH-SOUTH BOOKS
New York   London   Toronto   Melbourne

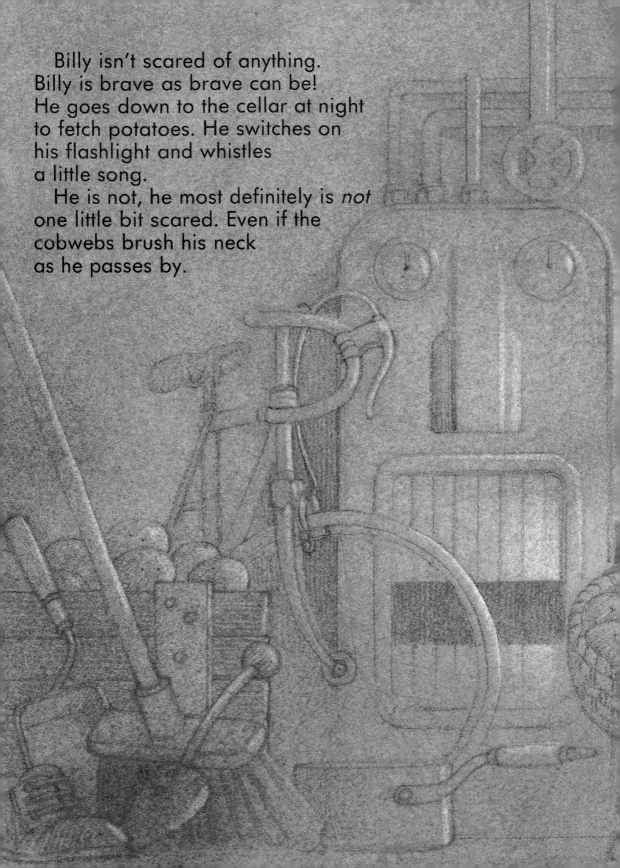

Billy isn't scared of anything.
Billy is brave as brave can be!
He goes down to the cellar at night
to fetch potatoes. He switches on
his flashlight and whistles
a little song.

He is not, he most definitely is *not*
one little bit scared. Even if the
cobwebs brush his neck
as he passes by.

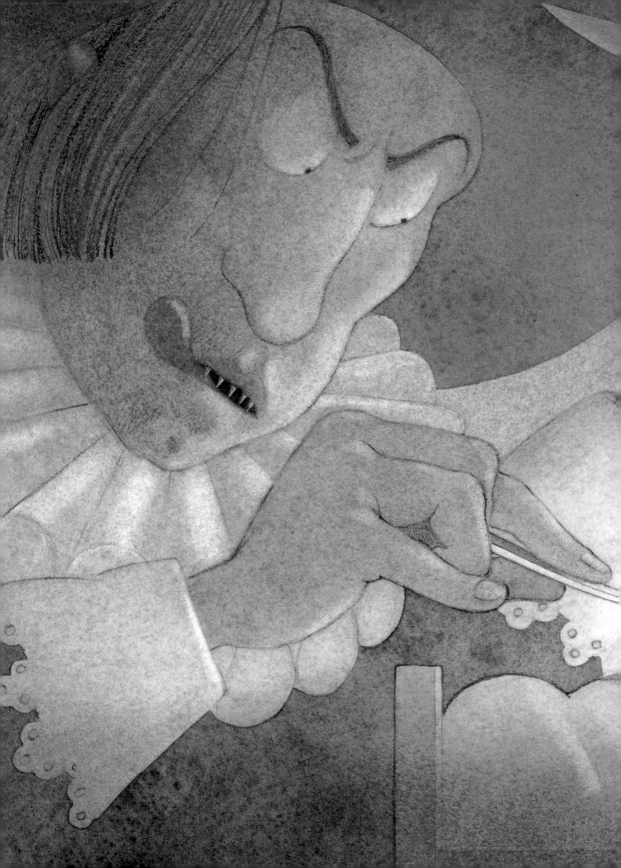

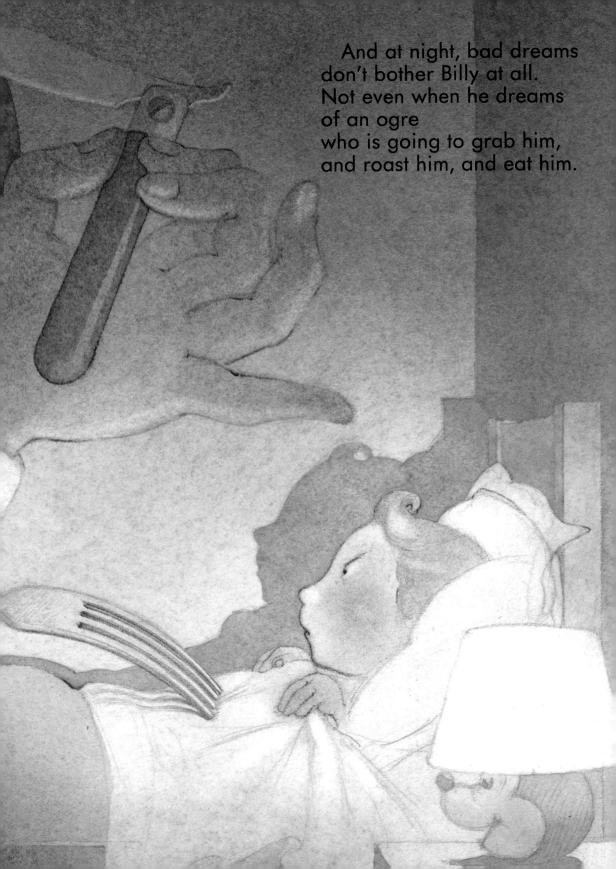

And at night, bad dreams
don't bother Billy at all.
Not even when he dreams
of an ogre
who is going to grab him,
and roast him, and eat him.

Billy just says,
"That's quite enough of that,
you great big lump!"
And BOING! He punches
the ogre right on the nose
and the ogre falls down flat.
So much for ogres.

On summer evenings
Billy often goes out
walking with his father.
It is very, very dark.
You can hardly see anything;
but that's the way Billy likes it.

Once he saw a shadow
lurking behind a bush,
and heard the sound
of footsteps behind a rock.

Billy just pushed the rock
with one finger, and WHAM!
It squashed the shadow's feet.
Billy never saw or heard
that shadow again.

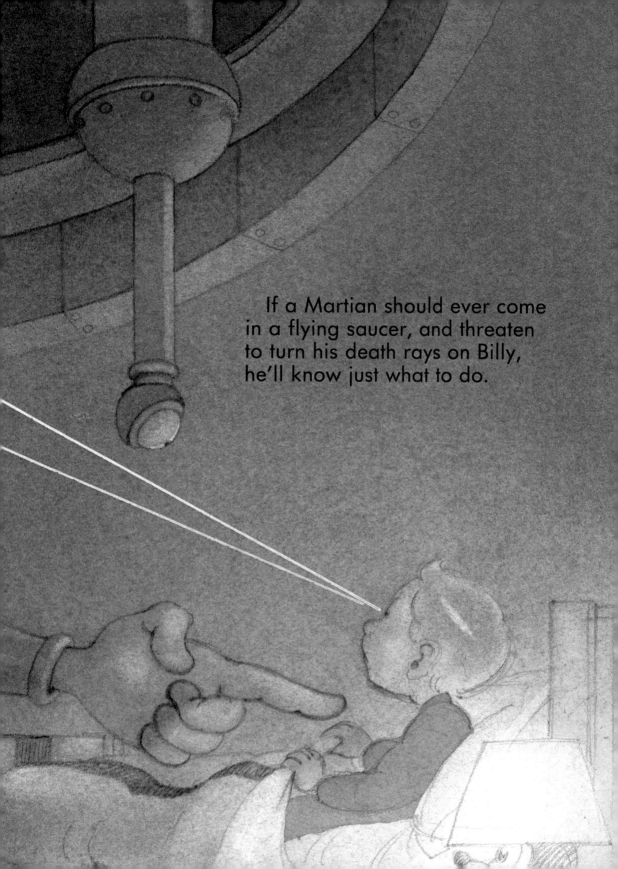

If a Martian should ever come in a flying saucer, and threaten to turn his death rays on Billy, he'll know just what to do.

Billy will just stare back at him so fiercely
that he'll lose his nerve and go all soft.
Billy can outstare anybody.
So much for death rays!

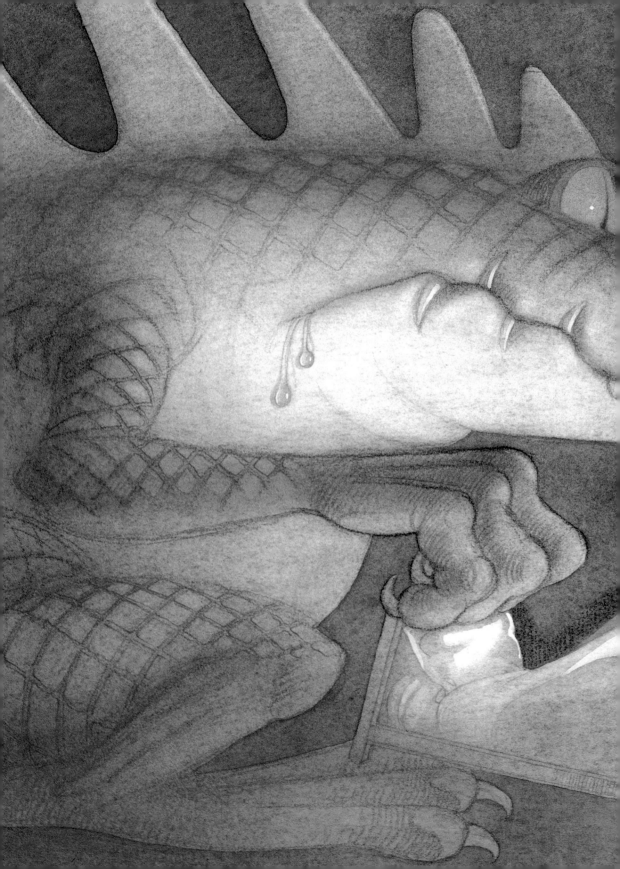

One day something was behind his bed.
He turned around and saw
a huge green monster
with sharp teeth and long claws.

Billy ran like the wind,
and slammed his bedroom door
right in that monster's face. WHAM!
The monster yelled because
he'd caught his paw in the door.
And he never came back.

Billy is the bravest boy
in the whole world.
When he comes home
and opens the door
with his own key,
because his mother and
father aren't home yet,
he isn't a bit scared
to be all alone in
the house.
Even if there
happen to be two
burglars hiding
in the room.

Billy will just knock them out, tie them up,
and telephone the police.
"Hi, this is Billy the Brave.
I just knocked out two burglars.
Please come and pick them up."

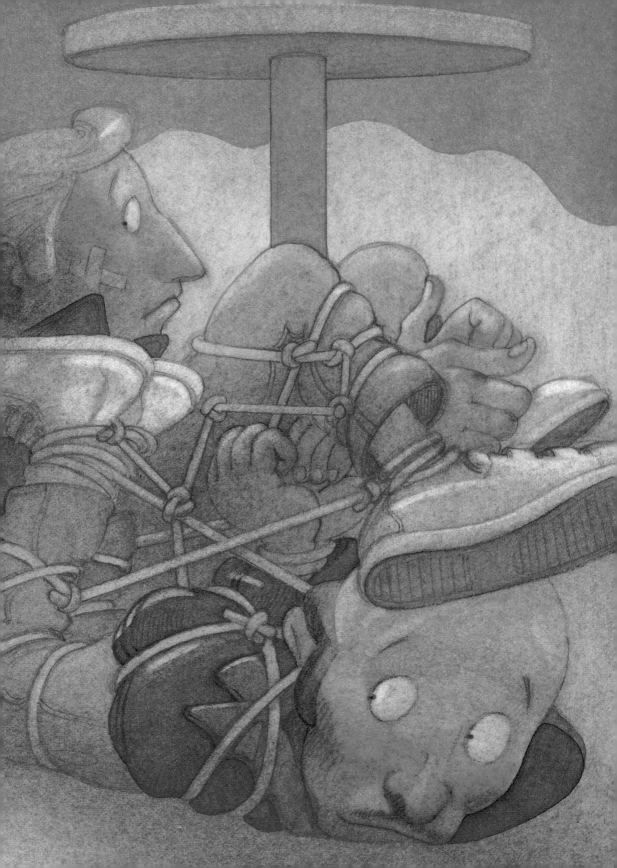

No, Billy isn't scared of anything.
But when he goes to bed,
he says to his mother:
"Please leave the light on in the corridor."
Not that Billy's afraid of the dark,
but it's nice to be able to see,
just in case any horrible monster
happens to drop in tonight...